For Antigone - Dan

For Rosalie - Ian

ISBN: 978-1-7398262-0-8

THE LEGEND OF THE KNIGHTWATCH

The Bear's Tale

Written by
Dan Baker

Illustrated by
Ian G Beck

There is a secret order who watch over us,
it appears. Unlikely knights, who have sworn,
to defend children from their fears.

And this is the tale of the knight who was told
he was too small. A brave, determined, teddy
bear whose quest did start it all.

Over many years, he saw his owners wake in fright...

tormented by the shadow beasts,

who lurk around at night.

The shadow beasts brought terrible dreams, that scared poor children awake.

But all he could do was simply watch, which made his big heart ache.

"We have to stop them," he did plea, "We have to make a stand."
But not one toy would join him on a quest to their dark land.

But Bear could not just sit on by, a calling he could hear.
So this small bear set off alone, to face the beast of fear.

He followed west the setting sun, in search of the twilight sea.

To sail across to their dark land, where he knew the beast would be.

But as he reached the shoreline, a small man was waiting there.
A friendly golden wizard, with a warm smile for the bear.

"I am the Sandman," he declared, "the creator of dreams so dear."
"I can do this alone no more. I need your help, I fear..."

"I use the sand to make good dreams, but the beach is getting less."

"The Shadow Beast grows more and more. This has turned into a mess."

"I knew of your arrival, Bear, for the sands did tell me true."

"An unlikely knight with such great heart would come - and that is you!"

"But I am just a bear," he said, "you really can't mean me?"
The Sandman gave a knowing smile, he knew Bear's destiny.

"Take a boat and sail to them, my brave and fearless knight.
Where you're going is so dark, you'll need the Sword of Light."

With that he muttered some magic words, raising his small hands. A beam of light burst from the ground, summoned from the sands.

"The Sword of Light will protect you and guide you beyond nightfall. It shows the truth behind these beasts, they're nothing real at all."

With that the bear was knighted and set off from the beach.
Under a sky of red and gold, the shadow lands in reach.

Soon the darkness was around him, but Bear pushed on as before.
The Sword of Light now guiding him safely, on towards the shore.

There he entered a haunting wood, trees twisted, bent and black.
Where creatures watched him from afar and plotted their attack.

Bear began to doubt himself, "A knight should not feel dread!"

But then he heard a cry for...

HELP!

...from somewhere up ahead.

Not thinking, he charged forward, the light made the creatures flee,
leaving a frightened zebra cowering behind a tree.

The zebra said "Oh thank you! I was completely overthrown.
They saw that I was terrified of being on my own."

"But now I can see clearly, that this terror and ordeal,
were just my little worries and the shadows are not real."

The zebra said his name was Grey, although he was black and
white. He asked if he could join Bear's quest - the steed for this
bright knight.

Bear thought this was very kind, it made him feel more brave.
And soon they found a clearing with an entrance to a cave.

This was where the Shadow Beast was waiting, deep below.
Grey and Bear's fears and doubts began to grow and grow.

It's true that this small bear was scared, but a promise he did swear.

He raised the magic Sword of Light and entered the pitch-dark lair.

The beast rose from the shadows as the bear stepped into sight.
He raised himself to his grand size, to give the bear a fright.

The beast declared "I know you're scared, it's something I can feel!"

The Sword of Light began to blink, its light started to fade.
The Shadow Beast smiled a nightmare grin...

"Admit it. You're afraid!"

"Your fear just gives me power! I'm sorry, you've been misled!
That torch cannot protect you, it's powers are in your head."

Suddenly Bear realised, the truth he had to find, was that all the scary shadow beasts are only in our mind.

With that a magic shield appeared in a blinding flash of light. It made the Shadow Beast recoil, his power replaced with fright.

"You magnify our worries," the knight said with a stare.

"You twist them into nightmares, to frighten and to scare."

Bear looked at Grey and nodded, "The light reveals what's true."

"Because we know that they're not real...

we're not afraid of you!"

With that the beast shrank away and vowed "I will return..."
"There will always be a child out there with worry or concern."

"And we will always be nearby," the knight and zebra swore.
"So you can't try to scare each child, the way you did before."

The legend says that from that day, the woods began to flower.
The truth discovered by that small bear decreased the beast's
dark power.

The story of a small brave knight, soon spread across the land.
One who faced the Shadow Beast, with sword and shield in hand.

"You saved the beach!" the Sandman smiled, "But there is more to do.
The sands tell me that you must find others, brave like you!"

"Find those of heart..."

"and those of strength..."

"the courageous, and the wise..."

"those who will protect their children, no matter what their size."

Bear and Grey set off once more, for heroes never rest,
to find other brave adventurers who'll join their noble quest.

So as you settle down to sleep, a good knight watches on.
Ready to dispel bad dreams, until the night is gone.

And the quest goes on for our small bear, as he rides his zebra, Grey.

Throughout the worlds of dreams and fears, they'll keep shadow beasts at bay.

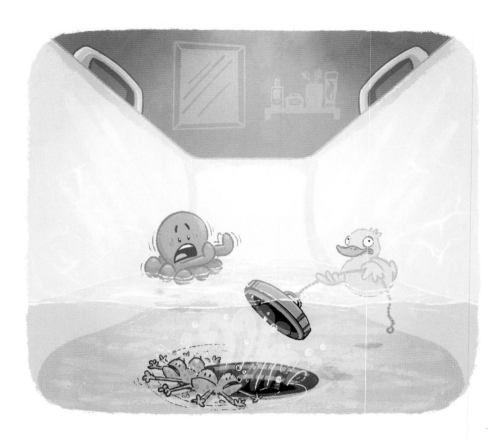

There will be more legends for us to share,
of monsters and other things that scare.

For as long as there are things to fear,
the Knightwatch Order will be here.

Printed in Poland
by Amazon Fulfillment
Poland Sp. z o.o., Wrocław

15784114R00020